Izzy the Inventor
and the Time-Travelling Gnome

USBORNE QUICKLINKS

DISCOVER EXPERIMENTS LIKE THE ONES IZZY TRIES IN THIS BOOK AND FIND OUT MORE ABOUT THE SCIENCE BEHIND THEM...

AT USBORNE QUICKLINKS WE HAVE PROVIDED LINKS TO WEBSITES WHERE YOU CAN:

• Make your own noisy inventions.

• Learn to fold paper to create a jumping frog.

• Explore the science of sound.

• Find lots more experiments to try at home.

TO VISIT THESE SITES, GO TO USBORNE.COM/QUICKLINKS AND TYPE IN THE KEYWORDS "IZZY AND THE TIME TRAVELLING GNOME" OR SCAN THE QR CODE ON THIS PAGE.

PLEASE FOLLOW THE INTERNET SAFETY GUIDELINES AT USBORNE QUICKLINKS.

CHILDREN SHOULD BE SUPERVISED ONLINE.

USBORNE

Izzy the INVENTOR

and the Time-Travelling Gnome

Zanna Davidson

ILLUSTRATED by ELISSA ELWICK

contents

Meet Izzy

She wants to be the...

Greatest Inventor

of **ALL** time.

Izzy always believed in **SCIENCE**, *not* magic. But then, one day, something unexpected happened. A fairy appeared in her bedroom, saying...

It is I, Rose Petal Twinkle-Toes, your Fairy Godmother.

The fairy gave Izzy a unicorn (which she hadn't asked for)...

...and sent her on a mission to Fairytale Land (which she didn't believe in).

From that moment on, life for Izzy would never be the same again...

7

CHAPTER ONE
Where Is A Fairy When You Need One?

Izzy was in bed, reading the last page of her fairy tale book. And what she read **DIDN'T** sound good...

Henry the Unicorn, her BEST FRIEND in *Fairytale Land*, was in trouble...

The wicked **Bad Fairy Brenda** had locked him in a tower...

...and the tower was guarded by a giant,

a wolf

and a talking harp.

"Oh no!" thought Izzy, "I have to rescue Henry. I can't leave him in that tower..."

But to get to Fairytale Land, Izzy needed a fairy.

Where is a FAIRY when you need one?

Usually, when there was a Fairytale Land emergency, Fairy Rose Petal appeared in a sparkly pink mist.

Then, all Izzy had to do was go
THROUGH the mist to get there.

Izzy knew this sounded very
MAGICAL and not at all scientific...

But I am
working on
the *science*
part!

Izzy had written down her ideas in her **science notebook**. (It was never far from her side.)

SCIENCE AND MAGIC

A scientific paper by IZZY

Maybe magic is just science we don't understand yet! After all, lots of scientific things would seem MAGICAL if we didn't know how they worked:

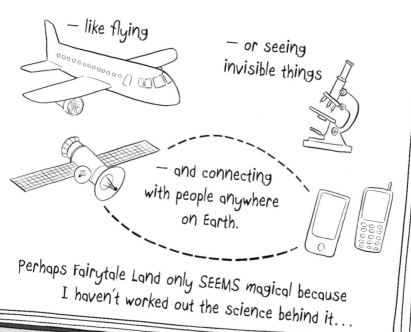

— like flying

— or seeing invisible things

— and connecting with people anywhere on Earth.

Perhaps Fairytale Land only SEEMS magical because I haven't worked out the science behind it...

Izzy spent the rest of the day looking for Fairy Rose Petal, but she was *nowhere* to be seen. She wasn't at **breakfast**...

...or **at school**...

And there was no sign of the fairy when she came **BACK HOME**.

"She's sure to turn up," Izzy decided. "I'll work on my **noisy** inventions while I wait for her. There are a few more in my notebook I want to try…"

IZZY'S NOISY INVENTIONS

Squeaky-Squealer

Fold a small rectangle of paper in half, fold the ends and then cut a V-shape out of the bottom. Place two fingers under these folds and blow, hard, towards the 'v'.

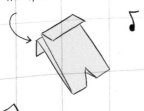

Pan pipes

Take six to eight drinking straws, cut to different lengths, and hold together with tape. Lift the pipes to your lips and blow...

Comb-onica

Fold a piece of baking paper around a comb. Touch the paper to your lips (with the comb's teeth facing you) and hum.

Works best when your lips are dry!

Tin pan drums

Put baking paper over a saucepan and keep it in place with string or a large elastic band. Then hit it with a spoon!

It sounds different depending on how tightly the paper is in place.

Boomer

Purse your lips, stick out your tongue and blow a raspberry down a tube.

If you hit the right note when you blow, it should BOOM!

Twanger

Place large elastic bands over an empty tissue box, like this. Then twang away!

Roarer

Stick a heavy coin to a strip of cardboard and thread a piece of string through the other end.

1. 2. 3.

Then swing it in a circle above your head. What a sound!

Whistle-Warbler

Roll a piece of thin card around a pencil to make a tube. Seal the sides with sticky tape.

Then blow across the tube (where the arrow is pointing) and slide the pencil up and down inside the tube at the same time. Now you're warbling!

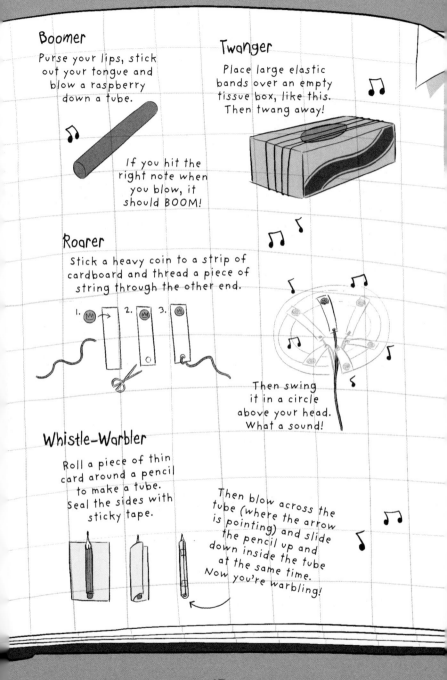

Izzy had just started playing her
latest **MUSICAL INVENTION** when Fairy
Rose Petal finally appeared.

At that exact same moment, her
little sister, Bella, burst through
her bedroom door.

"Izzy!" she cried. "You're magic! You played a tune and a fairy came! This is SO exciting!"

Izzy sighed. "That's not what happened. And a **SCIENTIST** never jumps to conclusions."

"What's more," Izzy went on, "the fairy is also **LATE**!" She turned to Fairy Rose Petal. "Where have you been? I need to get to 𝒯airytale ℒand to save Henry."

Fairy Rose Petal just shrugged.

"Fairytale Land? **UNICORNS!**" cried Bella. "This sounds **SO AMAZING.** Can I come? Please! It's not fair if you get to have all the fun!"

They need me for my SCIENCE SKILLS!

I can learn science!

But you HATE science!

I'll do anything if it means I can go to FAIRYTALE LAND.

"Fine," sighed Izzy. "You can come. I'll just pack us each a science bag."

My equipment...

Some of my latest noisy inventions – just in case...

Comb-onica

Boomer

Megaphone

Twanger

Pan pipes

Squeaky-Squealer

Roarer

Spoons

My accessories...

Magic map of Fairytale Land...

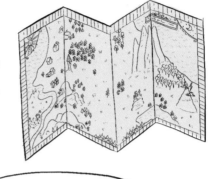

And, last but not least, my science notebook.

23

"Time for that sparkly mist, please, Fairy Rose Petal," said Izzy.

"Honestly," said Fairy Rose Petal. "All this rush. It's not like anything's going to happen to Henry in his tower. Here we go..."

The tower will be just on the other side of this mist.

But the tower **WASN'T THERE**.

Instead, there was a large pile of **stones**... and one very grumpy gnome.

"What's happened?" asked Izzy. "Where's Henry?"

"Pack of ogres," said the gnome. "On a rampage. You just missed them. They knocked down the tower!"

And I think that unicorn may well have been... squished.

CHAPTER TWO
The Time Machine

"Squished?" wailed Izzy.
"Henry can't be **SQUISHED**."

"And Rapunzel too," said the gnome. "She was in the tower as well, I'm afraid."

"Oh my goodness!" said Bella. "That's TERRIBLE! She's my favourite fairytale princess. *Poor Rapunzel!*"

She's supposed to live Happily Ever After!

"What about the wolf, the giant and the talking harp?" said Izzy. "They were meant to be guarding the tower!"

"They ran away," said the gnome. "I took shelter in my well."

"Oh dear," said Fairy Rose Petal. "This is a bit of a problem."

A BIT of a PROBLEM? It's a TRAGEDY! And it's all because you were LATE!

"I'm afraid I was caught up with something else," explained Fairy Rose Petal. "But don't worry Izzy. I know you can fix this. I have faith in you!"

Use your SCIENCE SKILLS! You can't be Izzy the Inventor for nothing. Ta-ta!

"You're leaving?" said Izzy.

"Yes," said Fairy Rose Petal. "You know – places to go, magical creatures to see. I'll come back and check on you later..."

And then PLINK! She was gone.

"That fairy's not what I was expecting," said Bella. "She wasn't exactly helpful, was she?"

"No," agreed Izzy. "Although she's not as awful as Bad Fairy Brenda – putting Henry in the tower in the first place."

"No one's worked out how to make a time machine yet," Izzy went on. "But there's no scientific law that says they're impossible..."

"Here – take a look in my science notebook."

Time Travel

A scientific paper by IZZY THE INVENTOR

We can travel back and forth in space,

so why not in time?

All you need is a wormhole — a tunnel between the present and the past. Then you could travel between the two!

Wormhole

PRESENT

<u>Problems with Time Travel:</u>

1. To time travel, you first need to find a wormhole. (Not quite sure how to do that!)

2. Then you'd need to stretch the wormhole, to make sure it's big enough.

3. Can you pass through a wormhole and survive? NOT SURE!!!

PAST

"We just have to solve a few problems," said Izzy. "Then we can **SAVE HENRY**..."

"I'm not at all sure about this," said Bella.

There was a loud, huffing noise from the gnome. "Isn't anyone going to ask ME for help?"

"They're not!" said Bella. "In
my world, people LOVE gnomes.
They have little statues of them
in their gardens."

"I don't want to be a statue!" said
the gnome. "I want to be in fairy
tales. Do you know ANY fairy tales
about gnomes?"

"Another dwarf," snapped the gnome. "There's only ONE fairy tale about a gnome and it's

REALLY BORING!"

It's all about arguing princes and a damp, dark well.

"I'm sorry about that," said Izzy, trying to calm the gnome down.

"Well," said the gnome, "it has meant I've had lots of time on my hands, to make myself useful..."

"You see," the gnome went on, "Izzy isn't the ONLY scientist in Fairytale Land. For I have invented a **time machine!**"

"Really?" cried Izzy.

"Yes!" said the gnome, proudly. "Follow me!" And he led them through a little clump of trees...

...past some thorn bushes...

...around the
house of a
little pig...

...around the
house of another
little pig...

...and then, suddenly, he stopped.

Ta da!

"This is your time machine?"
said Izzy.

It wasn't how she'd imagined
a time machine would look.

"Does it really work?" asked
Izzy. "Can you send us back to
before the ogres knocked down
the tower?"

41

The **time machine** started shaking.

"Have you ever done this before, Mr. Gnome?" asked Bella.

"Not exactly..." said the gnome.

42

The next moment, Izzy had
a horrible feeling...

...of being s-t-r-e-t-c-h-e-d

as the **time machine**

started zooming down

the wormhole.

Aaaaargh!!!!

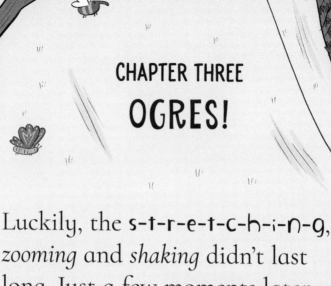

CHAPTER THREE
OGRES!

Luckily, the s-t-r-e-t-c-h-i-n-g, *zooming* and *shaking* didn't last long. Just a few moments later there was a loud **CLUNK**, then silence. They had landed.

Izzy and Bella stepped outside. "Hmm," said Izzy, studying her magic map. "Something has gone **WRONG!**"

LITTLE RED RIDING
HOOD'S COTTAGE

MERMAID SEA

LITTLE PIG'S
BRICK HOUSE

LITTLE PIG'S
STICK HOUSE

LITTLE PIG'S
STRAW HOUSE

WOODS FULL
OF BEARS AND
WOLVES

CINDERELLA'S
HOUSE

WISHING
WELL

RAPUNZEL'S
TOWER

DRAGON'S
LAIR

CAVE
OF GHASTLY
GOBLINS

TO JACK'S
BEANSTALK

FAIRYTALE LAND

ANOTHER SEA
(WITHOUT MERMAIDS)

OGRES
LIVE
HERE

HOME
TO
YET
MORE
OGRES

VERY
HIGH
MOUNTAINS

✗ YOU ARE HERE

INEDIBLE FOREST
(STILL THERE)

EDIBLE FOREST
(NO LONGER
THERE)

MOUNTAIN
OF DOOM

THE BEAST'S
CASTLE

BOTTOMLESS
LAKE OF DESPAIR

"And that's not all," said Izzy, looking through her telescope.

"Coming over those mountains are lots and lots of **MASSIVE OGRES!** They've already started their **rampage**."

"We'll never make it to the tower in time to rescue Henry," Izzy cried. "Or Rapunzel!" added Bella.

"Some people are never satisfied," snapped the gnome. "I've just taken you **BACK IN TIME...**"

"It's just that if we want to save Henry... *and Rapunzel*," Izzy went on, "we'll have to work out a way to **STOP** those ogres. Fast!"

"I can see them now," said Bella, looking through the telescope.

They're huge!

"And mostly made of stone," added the gnome.

"Mr. Gnome," said Izzy. "Do you know a way to stop them?"

"I think I've helped you enough," grunted the gnome.

"*Please*," said Izzy. "I'll do anything. I'll, um, give you my science kit!"

The gnome looked **UNMOVED**.

"Tell me," said Izzy. "What do you want?"

I want to be in a REALLY GOOD fairy tale.

"Don't you see," said Izzy. "Rapunzel's in that tower and hers is one of the most famous fairy tales of all. If you help us rescue Rapunzel, then you'll be part of her story."

Hmm. That's true. Okay, I do know one thing about ogres.

Ooh... what is it?

They really HATE water.

Izzy looked around and spotted a stream nearby. Her eyes lit up and she pulled out her **science notebook**. "I know what we need!

WATER BALLOONS!"

Make Your Own Water Balloons

by Izzy

What you need: square paper, scissors, pencil

1. Fold the paper in half, from top to bottom. Open out and then fold in half again, from left to right. Unfold.

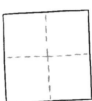

2. Fold the paper diagonally, from top left to bottom right. Unfold. Then fold again from top right to bottom left. Unfold.

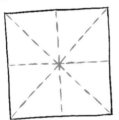

3. Fold the left horizontal crease down to the vertical crease.

Repeat on the right-hand side and then fold down the creases on both sides to make a triangle.

It should have two layers, like this:

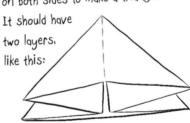

4. Fold up each of the bottom corners of the top layer to the top of the triangle.

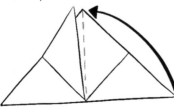

5. Fold the tips of the new triangles towards the middle.

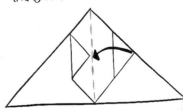

6. Take the top flap on the left-hand side and fold it down to the left, using the previous fold as a guide.

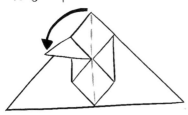

7. Now fold this new little triangle in half towards the middle (as shown by the dotted line).

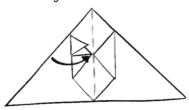

8. Lift the little triangle up and tuck it in the pocket below the triangle underneath.

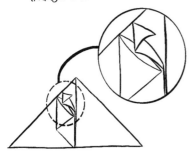

9. Repeat steps 6-7 for the right-hand side.

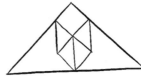

Turn the paper over and repeat steps 4-8 on the other side.

10. Then slide your fingers up the sides and open them out to form the shape shown below, so the flaps stick out in four different directions.

11. Push a pencil through the top hole to make it bigger. Remove the pencil and blow into the hole to inflate the paper into a little box. Fill it with water and throw it!

"And you call that **science?**" sniffed the gnome. "It sounds more like origami to me."

"Now we'd better get started,"
said Izzy. "We've no time to lose!"

"Hmm," said Izzy. And she started rifling through her **science notebook** again. "Aha!" she cried. "I have the solution to our problem!"

Catapults

What you need: Two sticks   Elastic bands

What to do:

- Cross two sticks as in the picture below.

- Then loop an elastic band around the middle to hold them in place.

- Cut a long, strong elastic band and tie an end to each of the twigs.

- Hold your object inside the elastic band, pull back and let it gooooooo!

"Catapults are science?" asked Bella. "Really?"

"*Everything* is science," said Izzy. "Now, let's find some sticks and make our catapults!"

My finger's stuck.

By the time they had prepared the catapults, they could hear the ogres' **THUNDERING** footsteps.

Then the ground **STARTED SHAKING**.

The sky went **dark**.

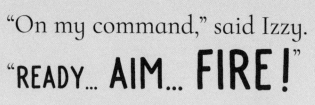

"On my command," said Izzy.
"READY... AIM... FIRE!"

As soon as the water balloons
hit the ogres, they started to
SHRINK.

They got
smaller...

and
smaller...

...and smaller.

"The ogres don't look very happy about it though," said Izzy. "Can I ever turn them back?"

Then Izzy collected up all the tiny ogres and popped them into her bag.

"And now," she said, "it's time to rescue Henry and Rapunzel. Because as soon as **Bad Fairy Brenda** finds out what's going on, she's sure to make things WORSE."

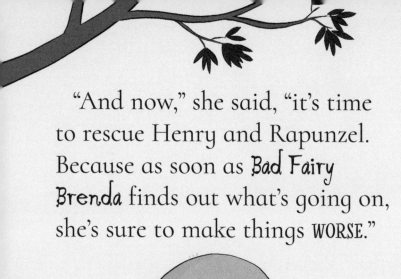

"Oops," said the gnome.
"What's the matter?" asked Izzy.
"I forgot to mention it..." said the gnome.
"But **Bad Fairy Brenda** has been checking on the tower every day at sunset..."

Izzy looked at
the sun, slipping
down through the sky.

"HURRY!" she said.

We need to get
to that tower
before Brenda!

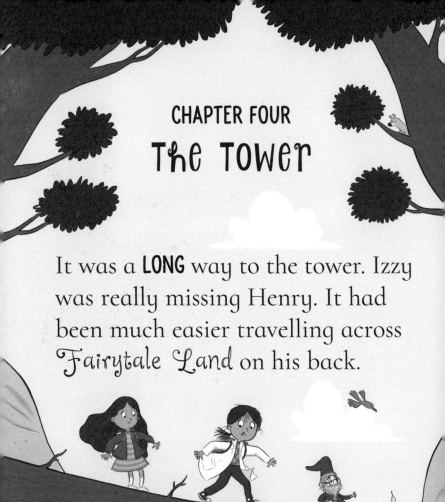

CHAPTER FOUR
THe TOWeR

It was a **LONG** way to the tower. Izzy was really missing Henry. It had been much easier travelling across *Fairytale Land* on his back.

But it wasn't *just* that, Izzy realized. She was missing Henry's enthusiasm...

...his dancing...

...and, most of all, his hugs.

When they finally reached the tower, Izzy, Bella and the gnome crouched down behind a nearby bush.

How are we going to get past them to rescue Henry and Rapunzel?

"If they see us, they're going to call on **Bad Fairy Brenda**. Which would be BAD," said the gnome.

"Luckily," said Bella proudly, "I've got a plan."

"*You've* got a plan?" said Izzy.

"You're not the only one who can think of things," retorted Bella. "My **fairy tale** knowledge can help us too!"

Giants love BEANSTALKS and don't like boys called Jack...

I know JUST how to deal with him!

Wolves are easily distracted by small people in red...

Bella and the gnome started whispering. Bella handed him her red jacket.

That just leaves the talking harp. Think you can handle him, Izzy?

Well... I'll, um, try.

Then Bella strode out from behind the bushes.

"Master! Master!" called the harp.
The giant opened **ONE EYE**.
Then the other. He sat up and **STARED** down at Bella.
Bella **GULPED**.

No!

The giant's face turned bright **red**. Then he stumbled to his feet and raced off in the direction of his beanstalk.

By now, though, the wolf was looking **hungrily** at Bella.

Don't eat ME! I know someone much tastier for you to eat. Over there!

"Little Red Riding Hood!" cried the wolf. And she shot off after the gnome.

"I can tell you two are up to **no good**," said the harp.

Izzy was about to
answer, when she heard
a cry from the sky.

Oh Izzy!
Is that really
you?

You came to
save me! I knew
you would!

Izzy looked up and
there was Henry at
the tower window.

A moment later, Rapunzel joined him. "Have you come to rescue us?" she asked.

My prince came earlier, but he rode off as soon as he spotted the giant.

"We just need to persuade the harp to let you go!" called Izzy. "**Never!**" said the harp.

"I'm calling **Bad Fairy Brenda** right now," the harp went on.

"Wait!" said Izzy, her mind whirring. *How was she going to persuade the harp?* Then, all of a sudden, it came to her...

Music! Wouldn't you love it if we all played music together?

Yes, I suppose I would. It gets quite lonely, being the only instrument here.

"If we all play music together, do you promise to let Rapunzel and Henry go?" asked Izzy.

"I do," said the harp.

Izzy proudly brought out her instruments.

Then Bella gathered up some fairytale creatures to make more music and Izzy explained how the instruments worked. By now, it was nearly sunset...

The gnome had also returned,
looking very pleased with himself.

"Ready, everyone?" said Izzy.
And they all began to play.

I'll join too, on my bottle pipes!

It was **BRILLIANT!**

Rapunzel was especially good on her bottle pipes, until Henry tried to join in.

"I'm having the best time **EVER**," said the harp. "So much so, that I've changed my mind. I'm not letting Henry and Rapunzel leave this tower. I want to do this **ALL NIGHT LONG**."

"Oh no!" thought Izzy. "My plan has gone horribly wrong." But just then...

...Henry started **to sing**.

La La Laaaaaaa!

La La Laaaaaaa! La La Laaaaaaa! La La Laaaaaaa! La La Laaaaaaa!

"**HOORAY!**" said Henry.
"We're saved."

**THEN HE LOOKED
DOWN.**

"But how are we
going to get
out of
here?"

CHAPTER FIVE
RAPUNZEL LETS HER HAIR DOWN

Bella gazed up at Henry in the tower. "Can't he just fly down," she said, "with Rapunzel on his back?"

"Don't panic," said Rapunzel. "I know *exactly* what to do. All I need is a pair of scissors."

"Now you get a starring role in a famous fairy tale!" Izzy told the gnome.

"You're right," said the gnome, his eyes shining. "And I've always wanted to say this..."

Rapunzel, Rapunzel, let down your hair!

Down it comes...

...and up I go!

When the gnome reached the top, Rapunzel cut off her hair...

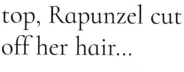

Snip! Snip!

...tied it to the window latch...

"Come on, Henry!" called Izzy. "We don't have long before Bad Fairy Brenda arrives."

"You can do this, Henry!" called Izzy. "I know you can."

Henry took a deep breath and hoped for the best...

"Oh, Henry," said Izzy. "It's so good to see you again."

"Thank you for saving me," said Henry.

And they gave each other a huge hug.

"I wasn't the only one who saved you," said Izzy. "Meet my sister, Bella. She helped, too. And Mr. Gnome, of course."

"You've all been wonderful," said Rapunzel. "And I can't tell you how much better I feel with shorter hair."

It's so light! And bouncy, too.

"There's just one thing I don't understand," said Bella, puzzled. "Why didn't you ask for a pair of scissors before?"

"In my fairy tale book," Bella went on, "the prince brings you a piece of silk each day."

"I thought it was important to keep to the story," said Rapunzel. "You know – to do things the way they'd always been done. But now I've changed my mind!"

My prince rode off as soon as he saw the giant. And that made me think...

Is it really a good idea to sit around waiting for someone to come and rescue you?

No! It's not! It's much better to change the story and save yourself!

97

"That's brilliant!" said Izzy. "And just like a **scientist!** You questioned things. You looked at the facts and you found a way to solve the problem."

Hooray for Rapunzel!

"It's quite scary though, changing your story," admitted Rapunzel. "I don't really know what to do now."

"I feel the same," said the gnome. "I've left my fairy tale, all about a boring Wishing Well. But now I've decided to go on lots of time-travelling adventures!"

"Another happy ending," said Henry, beaming. "Look at them, going off together into the sunset."

"**THE SUNSET?**" cried Izzy. "OH NO!"

The next moment there was a loud

BANG!

And a huge

FLASH!

And before you could say,

"Abracadabra!" Bad Fairy Brenda appeared before them.

Why, if it isn't Izzy and her little unicorn friend!

You're not getting away from me THIS TIME! Mwa ha ha haaa!

CHAPTER SIX
Standing UP TO BULLieS

"Well, smarty pants," snapped Brenda, "you've messed up my plans again! It's time to put a stop to you and your **INVENTIONS** once and for all."

Uh oh!

But as Izzy closed her eyes, wondering if Bad Fairy Brenda was about to turn her into a toad, she had a thought...

I know what Brenda is... She's a BULLY.

And the best way to deal with bullies is to STAND UP TO THEM!

"This has got to STOP, Brenda," said Izzy. "You're being a BIG BULLY and this time you went **TOO FAR!**"

Henry and Rapunzel were SQUISHED. It took a time-travelling gnome to save them.

"You can't go around behaving like this," Izzy went on. "I want you to apologise. **RIGHT NOW!**"

"And what's more," added Bella, "do you know what happens to BAD characters in fairy tales..?

Greedy wolves get **CHOPPED!**

Evil Queens are **BANISHED**.

And wicked witches end up in the **OVEN!**"

"That's actually a good point," said Bad Fairy Brenda. "Maybe I do need to re-think my life..." She turned to Henry. "Sorry," she mumbled.

"We can't hear you!" said Izzy.

"I think I need some time alone," said Brenda, "to think things over."

107

"Turns out she's not such a **bad fairy** after all!" said Henry. "Although what was that you said about me getting squished?"

Before Izzy could think what to say, there was a shower of stars...

...and in fluttered Fairy Rose Petal.

"Oh good! You saved Henry. Well done, Izzy," said Fairy Rose Petal. "I knew I could rely on you."

"Don't you see, Izzy?" said Fairy Rose Petal. "I'm teaching you about all the amazing things you can do!"

"I'd come if you really needed me," said Fairy Rose Petal, looking **SERIOUS** for a moment.

"And think of what you've discovered – that science really can change the world!"

"I've got one more question for you," said Izzy. "I still don't understand how Fairytale Land exists. Can you explain it?"

"Think of it this way," said Fairy Rose Petal, smiling. "It's like the great scientist, Michael Faraday, once said...

Nothing is too wonderful to be true..."

The world really is a magical place. And sometimes you just need to open your mind to see it...

"And now," she added, "it's time for you to go home."

> But I've hardly seen Henry...

> Never mind! I'm sure you'll be back soon.

Fairy Rose Petal waved her wand and soon they were surrounded by the sparkly pink mist once more.

Izzy and Bella walked through the mist...

...and moments later they were back in Izzy's bedroom, where it all began.

"**WOW!**" said Bella. "What an adventure. Thank you for letting me come too, Izzy. And maybe from now on, I could work on some of your inventions with you? I've decided science is quite **COOL** after all."

"You helped me too," said Izzy. "You tricked the **GIANT**...

...and the
WOLF...

...and you
helped with Bad
Fairy Brenda.

And you know what – it was FUN
going on an adventure together."

Then they heard their dad, calling
up the stairs. "Time for bed, girls."

Izzy yawned. "Pyjama time,"
she said. "Although I've got this
funny feeling I've forgotten
something. Let's just look at the
Book of Fairy Tales, to
make sure everything's okay."

Rapunzel

The Prince never did come to rescue Rapunzel so, with the help of a pair of scissors and a noble gnome, Rapunzel decided to rescue herself, instead.

Afterwards, Rapunzel and the gnome flew off in a time machine to have many exciting and nail-biting adventures.

Actually, that's an even better ending than before.

I think so too! Let's just check the last page.

Rapunzel

There was just ONE problem. From that day forward, the ogres were missing from Fairytale Land. And you might think that was a good thing. But, oh no! Fairytale Land had lost its balance. Without the ogres, everything started to go WRONG. Wolves and bears ran riot. Witches and wizards cast countless wicked spells. Goblins and trolls came out from their caves and made mischief...

"I *knew* I'd forgotten something!" cried Izzy. **"THE TINY OGRES... ...I PUt them in my bag."**

She **RUSHED** over to look.

Oh no, Bella. They've gone!

We HAVE to find them!

Izzy turned to Bella. "Everything is going wrong because of us! We have to find those ogres and get them back to *Fairytale Land...*"

Here are some sound experiments from Izzy's *science notebook...*

Izzy's SOUND INVENTIONS

What is sound?

Sounds are caused by tiny movements called vibrations that travel through the air and the things around us. When these vibrations reach our ears, we hear them as sounds.

Small vibrations make quiet sounds and large vibrations make louder ones.

Make A Megaphone

A step-by-step guide by Izzy

What you need:

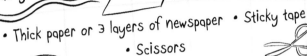

- Thick paper or 3 layers of newspaper
- Sticky tape
- Scissors

1. Cut a large square of thick paper or 3 layers of newspaper.

2. Roll the paper into a cone, then tape the edges together.

3. Snip off the small end to make a mouthpiece. Trim the large end, too, to make it even.

4. Now, speak or sing into the small end!

How it works:

Your voice (or music) echoes around the cone and makes the air inside vibrate a lot. This magnifies the sound, making it louder.

Create a sound tube

What you need:

- Cardboard tube with a bottom and a lid • Drawing pin
- Sharp pencil • Dried lentils or rice • Pens or pencils

1. Find a wide cardboard tube, with a lid. Use a drawing pin, then a sharp pencil to poke holes through the tube from one side to the other.

2. Slide pencils or pens into the holes, so they stick all the way through the tube. Pour some rice or lentils into the tube and put on the lid.

3. Turn the tube upside down. You should hear a pitter-patter noise like raindrops! When the sound stops, turn the tube over and listen again.

Make some bottle pipes

1. Arrange some different-shaped glass bottles in a row.

2. Pour water into them, filling them with different amounts. Blow over the mouth of each bottle.

Izzy's notes:

Blowing over the bottles makes the air in them vibrate, creating sounds. The type of sound you make depends on how much air there is. A little bit of air (in the bottles with more water) makes a higher sound. Lots of air (in the bottles with less water) makes a lower sound.

Extra sound tube facts:

As the grains slide along the tube, they bounce off the pencils or pens making them and the air in the tube vibrate. These bumps and bounces make the pitter-patter noise. You can change the sound by putting different things inside the tube — such as dried beans or beads.

Make a string telephone

What you need:

- Sharp pencil   • 2 empty plastic pots
  - Long piece of string

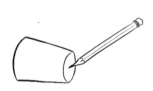

1. Use a sharp pencil to make a small hole in the base of two plastic pots.

2. Cut a very long piece of string. Thread one end through the hole in one of the pots and make a big knot inside.

Keep the string stretched tight and don't let it touch anything.

3. Fix the other end of the string in the other pot in the same way. Ask someone (maybe your unicorn friend) to take that pot into another room and hold it to one ear. Speak into your pot. Can the other person or unicorn hear you?

Izzy's notes:

Speaking into the pot makes the air inside it vibrate. The pot picks up the vibrations, which travel along the string. The other pot passes the vibrations back into the air so they can be heard again as sounds.

SCIENCE SAFETY

ALWAYS TAKE EXTRA CARE WITH HOT OR SHARP THINGS
AND NEVER PUT ANYTHING IN YOUR MOUTH. IF AN
ACTIVITY INVOLVES DOING SOMETHING YOU MIGHT NOT
USUALLY DO, ASK YOUR GROWN UP TO HELP YOU.

Series designer: Brenda Cole
Series editor: Lesley Sims
Cover design by Freya Harrison
and Hannah Cobley
Digital manipulation by Nick Wakeford